GIRLS
Contents

Rachel   *Ellie*

CHAPTER 1

My Room, My Palace

It's Saturday afternoon and Rachel
is at home. She hears the doorbell
and rushes downstairs to answer it.
As she swings open the door, she's
excited to see her best friend Ellie
standing there.

Rachel "Hi! Come in. Bring your
bag to my room. You've got to see
this!"

Rachel runs upstairs to her
bedroom, with Ellie only a few
steps behind.

Ellie "Oh wow! Cool! It doesn't even look like your room. It should be in one of those home magazines. I love the purple walls and those bright pink pillows—mad!"

Rachel "You should get your parents to paint your room for your birthday. I love birthdays, they're the best!"

Ellie "So what did you get?"

Rachel "Well, you know how I said my brother has been really mean to me lately?"

Ellie "Yes."

Rachel "Well, Dad made him promise to be nice to me for *the whole day*."

Ellie "Really? I'd like to see that!"

Rachel "Yes, right! So Dad said he's got to do the housework all by himself!"

Ellie "Imagine if your dad said your brother had to be our own personal slave for the day. And we could give him orders. Like princesses in a castle. Now that would be great!"

Rachel "Yes. I'd tell him to get us drinks and food every five minutes, and bow every time he spoke to us."

Ellie "Or get him to do tricks for us like a circus performer, or make him put on make-up and stand on his head."

Rachel "And I'd definitely make him play the music we like, not that head-banging rubbish he plays."

The girls break into giggles.

CHAPTER 2

Brotherly Hate

Rachel and Ellie are chatting in Rachel's room, planning what they'll do during the night.

Ellie "So, what else did you get for your birthday? Any Kylie or Beyonce?"

Rachel "Yes, both!"

Rachel picks up two CDs from her desk and waves them at Ellie.

Ellie "Doesn't Kylie look great?"

Rachel "Mmmm. Just imagine having all her clothes. How cool would we look! Hey, I've got an idea!"

Ellie "Another moment of brilliance? What's on your mind?"

Rachel "Well, my sister has just bought some new clothes and she's away for the whole weekend."

Ellie "Go on—I know what you're thinking."

Rachel "Exactly! But let me check Jay isn't around. If he catches us, he'll tell Mum and Dad because he knows I'm not allowed in my sister's room when she's not around."

Rachel opens the bedroom door
and quietly creeps up the hallway to
her sister's room. Her brother Jay is
nowhere to be seen. Rachel waves at
Ellie to come. They hurriedly grab
clothes out of the wardrobe then
sprint back to Rachel's room,
giggling nervously.

Ellie "Phew! We made it. Wow, your sister has such awesome clothes. I can't wait until I'm old enough to buy my own things."

Rachel "Here Ellie, try on this spotty top. It really matches your eyes. And I'll try the vest top and mini skirt. Here's some music to get us into the mood."

Rachel puts on one of her new CDs
and turns up the volume. She and
Ellie grab bracelets and other fake
jewellery from her dressing table,
then begin to dance to the music.
Suddenly Rachel spins around.

Rachel "What are you doing in
   here? Get out!"

Ellie also turns to find Rachel's
older brother, Jay, standing in the
doorway, smirking.

CHAPTER 3

Karaoke

Rachel glares sideways at her brother, looking really unimpressed.

Rachel "Mum! Jay's in my room!"

Rachel's mum doesn't answer as she's outside. So the girls scream at Jay until he leaves.

Rachel "Boy, that was close. And he didn't even realise we had my sister's clothes on. He can be so thick sometimes. We'd better get out of these clothes. What do you want to do then?"

Ellie "Let's try out your new karaoke machine."

Ellie "I love this song. Bags being Kylie. She's so cool!"

Rachel "You know she's nearly forty years old, or maybe over forty."

Ellie "That's ancient! That's as old as my mum, but Kylie's still cool, isn't she?"

Rachel "Well yes, she's Kylie! Right, I'm going to do a Robbie Williams song."

Ellie "And I'll do a Beyonce song."

Rachel "Great, you go first."

Rachel hands the microphone to Ellie and puts the karaoke CD in the player.

Rachel "Remember the words are on the screen."

Ellie begins to sing.

Rachel "Wow, Ellie, you're brilliant! You should try out for the next 'Pop Idol' or something. You sound amazing!"

Ellie (modestly) "Gee, thanks. But everyone sounds better with a good backing track."

Rachel looks up to see her brother clinging to the window ledge while he balances on the branch of a tree. He's staring at Ellie in a dreamy way, then loses his balance. When the girls rush over to the window, they see him dangling from a lower branch three metres off the ground.

CHAPTER 4

Zombie Boys

The two girls sit down on the floor in Rachel's room and continue chatting.

Ellie "Jay's lucky your dad was there to help him before he fell."

Rachel "But not that lucky! He got into big trouble and had to rake up all of the leaves that were under the tree."

Both girls laugh at the sight of Jay with the rake in his hand, looking like he is trying to break the world record for the slowest raking.

Ellie "I feel sorry for him, not!"

Rachel notices Ellie blushing.

Rachel "Sorry? Why, do you like my
brother or something, because if
you do, it's pretty obvious that he
likes you too!"

Ellie "Well, he's sort of cute, but I
think it'd be too weird to go out
with my best friend's brother."

Rachel "That's for sure! But if you did, you could come over all the time and be part of the family."

Ellie "Cool."

Rachel "Anyway, he probably just likes you because he likes your singing. He was mes ... mesmer ... What's that word that means when someone stares at you like they're in a trance? Like some zombie?"

Ellie "I think you mean, 'mesmerised'."

Rachel "Yes, that's it, mesmerised. My pathetic brother was mesmerised by your singing. Hey, wouldn't it be great if every time you sang, my brother turned into a zombie? Like it was some magical power you had over him."

Ellie "Yes, that would be so funny."

Rachel "But imagine if you could make every boy turn into a zombie. They would all follow you round like that Pied Piper and rats story."

Ellie "That would be totally cool but there would be one problem. You wouldn't be able to tell if they were zombies or not. Boys always look like zombies to me!"

They give each other "high fives" and collapse in a fit of giggles.

CHAPTER 5

Double Dare

Later that evening, the girls get into their pyjamas.

Rachel "Mum just called out that we've got half an hour until lights out. Do you want to play a game?"

Ellie "What sort of game?"

Rachel "Truth or Dare."

Ellie "Um, I'm not sure …"

Rachel "Come on. Truth or dare?"

Ellie "OK, truth."

Rachel "Um, let's see. Have you ever … picked your nose in the bath? And you said 'truth', so you can't lie."

Ellie blushes.

Rachel (squealing) "You have! Yuk, gross!"

Ellie "OK, but it was when I
was only three. I didn't know any
better. Now it's your turn and I'm
going to get you back, big time."
Rachel "OK, I'm choosing 'dare'."

Ellie "Cool. I dare you to go to your brother's room and say, 'I think you're great and as my brother, I really love you'."

Rachel "Now that's gross! *No way!*"

Ellie "You said 'dare' so you've got to do it. Unless you're 'chicken'."

Rachel hesitates then makes her
way to her brother's room. She
knocks on his door. He answers and
grunts, 'what?'

Rachel "I just wanted to say that …
Ellie is totally in love with you!"
Ellie "No!!! You're dead, Rachel."

Rachel rushes back to her room, laughing all the way up the hall. Rachel's mother calls upstairs for the girls to settle down and get ready to go to sleep.

Ellie "You know, I've had the best time. Can't wait for you to come to my place next time."

A few moments pass in the darkness.

Rachel "So did you really pick your nose in the bath?"

Rachel and Ellie once again break out laughing and don't stop until well into the night.

GIRLS ROCK!

Sleepover Lingo

Rachel

Ellie

accessories The extra things you wear when you dress up, such as bangles, necklaces, hairclips and handbags.

diva A top-selling female singing star, such as Kylie, Beyonce or Jamelia.

jim jams A slang word for pyjamas. Other names are PJs or jarmies.

karaoke A form of singing where someone sings a song in front of an audience. They follow the lyrics on a screen and sing to pre-recorded music.

lurve The way you say "love" when you really mean it, especially when you talk about someone being "in lurve".

GIRLS ROCK!
Sleepover Must-dos

⭐ Invite your best friends over for a sleepover at least once a month.

⭐ When your friends sleep over, make a sign that says "KEEP OUT! ESPECIALLY BOYS!" and stick it on your bedroom door.

⭐ Make sure you have some good CDs at your sleepover, so that you can dance and sing along to them.

⭐ Ask your friends who are sleeping over to bring some accessories to play with, such as bracelets and hairclips (or borrow your sister's).

⭐ Have plenty of food hidden in your room for your guests.

⭐ Make sure you have some recent magazines so you can read up on all the music and TV gossip.

⭐ Pretend you are stars. Make up your own band and have someone as the lead singer.

⭐ Remember to wear your favourite pyjamas and slippers.

⭐ Have some extra pillows in your bedroom—for pillow fights!

⭐ Once everyone has arrived, play "Truth or Dare".

Sleepover Instant Info

"Truth or Dare" is one of the most popular games played at sleepovers.

Some people wear big shirts called nightshirts to bed.

Many pillows are stuffed with goose feathers so they're really soft. Some are made from foam rubber and are more bouncy.

Lots of people snore in their sleep because their throat muscles are fully relaxed.

Sleeping Beauty slept for over a hundred years before being brought back to life by the kiss of a prince.

One of the seven dwarfs in the story "Snow White and the Seven Dwarfs" is called Sleepy.

Bears sleep in their caves for an entire winter—this is called hibernation.

There is a popular book and television series called "The Sleepover Club".

Think Tank

1 What does it mean when you choose "truth" in the game Truth or Dare?

2 Most sleepovers happen during the day. True or False?

3 Name one item you definitely need at a sleepover?

4 What is karaoke?

5 Who are the best people to invite to a sleepover?

6 Who is Kylie?

7 At a sleepover, should you share secrets with your friends?

8 What is the most popular clothing to wear at a sleepover?

Answers

8 The most popular clothing to wear is pyjamas and slippers.

7 Most definitely. It's the best place to share and find out about secrets!

6 Kylie is a pop star from Australia.

5 The best people to invite to your sleepover are your best friends of course!

4 Karaoke is when you sing with backing tracks and follow the words of the song on a screen.

3 You need to bring any of these items: pillows, sleeping bags, food, music, magazines.

2 False. They happen at night when most people sleep. Get it? Sleepover.

1 When you choose "truth", you have to tell the truth and nothing but the truth when asked a personal question.

How did you score?

- If you got 8 answers correct, you're ready to have your own sleepover. So, starting planning it now!

- If you got 6 answers correct, you'll probably be invited to a sleepover soon, so you might want to buy some new PJs before you go.

- If you got fewer than 4 answers correct, you prefer to get a good night's sleep at home.

Hey Girls!

I hope that you have as much fun reading my story as I've had writing it. I loved reading and writing stories when I was young. Some of my favourites really sparked my imagination and took me into weird and wonderful worlds.

Here are some suggestions to help you enjoy reading even more than you do now. At school, why don't you use "The Sleepover" as a play? You and your friends can be the actors. Get some pyjamas and slippers for your costumes and bring in some CDs and magazines to use as props.

So ... have you decided who is going to be Ellie and who is going to be Rachel? And what about the narrator?

Now act out the story in front of your friends. I'm sure you'll all have a great time! You might also like to take this story home and get someone in your family to read it with you. Maybe they can take on a part in the story.

So have as much fun with your reading as a monkey has in a banana plantation!

And remember, Girls Rock!

GIRLS ROCK!

When We Were Kids

Julie   Holly

Julie talked with Holly, another *Girls Rock!* author

Holly "Hey Julie, don't you come from a big family of singers?"

Julie "Yes, we all used to sing around the piano."

Holly "Did you fight over who was the best?"

Julie "We did, and it always bugged me that my brother could sing without taking a breath."

Holly "Maybe he was practising to be a deep sea diver."

Julie "Or he was just full of hot air!"

GIRLS ROCK!
What a Laugh!

Q Why did the girl take a pencil to the sleepover?

A So that she could draw the curtains!

GIRLS ROCK!

Read about the fun
that girls have in these
GIRLS ROCK! titles:

The Sleepover

Pool Pals

Bowling Buddies

Girl Pirates

Netball Showdown

School Play Stars

Diary Disaster

Horsing Around

GIRLS ROCK! books are available from
most booksellers. For mail order information
please call Rising Stars on 0870 40 20 40 8 or visit
www.risingstars-uk.com